D0417058

ALFRED
AND THE
VIKINGS

by Damian Harvey and James Rey Sanchez

W
FRANKLIN WATTS
LONDON•SYDNEY

ALFRED
AND THE
VIKINGS

CONTENTS

CHAPTER 1

A KING'S PROMISE

My name is Edwen, son of Egbert the blacksmith.

My father's skill was known throughout the land. People

travelled for many miles for him to shoe their horses

and make tools for them to farm the land. But his greatest

skill was crafting swords. The swords my father made

were the strongest and sharpest in the land. He was

sword maker for many kings and brave Saxon warriors.

When Ethelred, King of Wessex, wanted a new sword, he came to my father's forge. I was only seven years old but I remember it as if it were yesterday. The king arrived on horseback with his younger brother, Alfred. Running beside them were two of the biggest hunting hounds I'd ever seen. I hid behind my father's legs when the dogs came bounding in, but Alfred called them to his side with a sharp whistle. Whilst my father spoke to King Ethelred, Alfred beckoned me over and let me stroke the two hounds. As I ran my hands over their long grey coats, the hounds sat peacefully, resting their heads on our feet.

"I think they like you," said Alfred. "They are fierce hunting hounds, but they are clever, too. They know who they can trust."

"What would they do if I was an enemy?" I asked.

"They would attack," Alfred replied.

"Our swords will be ready in a few days," King Ethelred said to Alfred, slapping him on the shoulder as he went past. Ruffling my hair, Alfred got to his feet and followed his brother into the yard. They untied the horses and rode off, the hounds following alongside.

Some weeks later, Father was busy preparing the forge and laying out pieces of metal ready for the day's work. I was busy helping him when suddenly the peace and quiet of the morning was broken by the ringing of the church bell – an attack warning. The village erupted into a frenzy of activity. People were running everywhere, gathering children and heading towards the protection of the church. In the distance the sounds of shouting and screaming could be heard.

"Quickly!" cried my father, taking me by the hand, "we need to run and hide." No sooner had we stepped out into the sunlight, than my father stopped in his tracks. A little way ahead of us, a small group of warriors were making their way along the road. Each of the warriors had a round wooden shield, some carried them in their hands and some wore them slung across their backs. One or two wielded axes whilst others had swords or spears. Two had bows, with arrows notched and ready to fire. I'd never seen Viking warriors before but had heard enough stories to be sure that is what they were.

Running back to the forge, Father ushered me into a corner where he kept stacks of dry wood for the fire. "Here," he said, pointing to the woodpile. "Hide in there and don't make a sound until I come back to get you." I squeezed myself into a space amongst the wood. Father threw an old blanket over me to keep me hidden from view. From my hiding place, I listened to him moving around, clattering pieces of metal and then I heard the sound of feet approaching.

"Greetings," I heard my father say.

The voice that answered was rough and difficult to understand. I only managed to pick out a few words but it was enough for me to know that they wanted my father to make something for them. Father tried to explain that the metal laid out in the forge was already set aside for other people and he didn't have enough to spare.

This made the other man angry and he started shouting. My father argued back for a moment but suddenly I heard a heavy thud. My father let out a groan and then he was silent. The sound of laughter and footsteps receded as the Vikings went away. I stayed hidden in the darkness, not daring to move.

CHAPTER 2
RETURN OF THE KING

I don't know how long I stayed there in my dark, cramped hiding place but eventually the sound of horses' hooves reached my ears. I could hear voices talking and the sound of heavy footsteps as someone approached. I was sure that the Viking warriors had returned and a shiver of fear ran through my body.

The footsteps stopped close to my hiding place …
so close that I could hear the sound of heavy breathing. Carefully, I reached out and grasped a thick piece of wood to use as a weapon, though I knew it would be no defence against the Vikings. Suddenly, the blanket covering me was snatched away and I found myself looking up at a familiar face. It was Alfred, the king's brother.

"Come on boy," said Alfred, holding his hand out to me.

"You're safe now."

Alfred picked me up and carried me out of the forge,

holding me close so I could not see my father's body

as we passed. I later learnt that the Vikings had killed

anyone in the village that had stood in their way,

my parents among them.

As we rode along, Alfred told me he had never paid

my father for the swords, but instead had agreed that

I would be Alfred's squire when I was old enough.

To become a squire I would have to know how to clean and look after weapons and armour. I would also have to prepare Alfred's horse for battle and many other things. But just as importantly, I would need to know how to read and write. Alfred was very firm about this.

Alfred told me that when he was young, his mother would read poems from her favourite book to him and his brothers. "Then one day," said Alfred, "Mother told us that whichever one of us could learn the poems would be given the book as a prize." Even though he'd been the youngest, Alfred had been determined to win the book. He read poems each day before he got up and again before he fell asleep until he knew each one by heart. His mother had been overjoyed to hear him recite the poems and she kept her promise, giving him her much loved book. A book Alfred kept with him at all times.

"Being able to read and write is very important," said Alfred. "These are the things that will bring the people together as one. And that is why you will need to learn to read and write too."

Alfred also told me about his travels across the sea as a young boy. He described the magnificent streets of Rome and how the Pope himself had declared that one day Alfred would become king. Alfred smiled at this.

"Of course, it won't happen," he said. "Ethelred's son will be the next king, even if he is only a small boy."

Alfred was a good teacher and he taught me many things, but as time passed more and more of his time was being taken up fighting the Vikings. A new Viking warlord named Guthrum had risen up and was pushing the Saxons out of their lands. It seemed that the Vikings might take control of all Saxon land, but King Ethelred and Alfred did not give up.

In a fierce and bloody battle, Ethelred and Alfred managed to push the invaders back. It was a great victory but many lives were lost and the king himself was badly wounded. Alfred prayed by his brother's bedside day and night, but there was nothing he or anyone else could do to save him. When Ethelred died it was decided that, since his sons were but small boys, Alfred would be crowned King of Wessex. After all, as Alfred told me, children would be no use in defeating the Viking invaders.

CHAPTER 3
A SURPRISE ATTACK

By the time I was fourteen I had become King Alfred's squire, helping him with his armour, tending his horse and doing anything else asked of me. I like to think that my father would have been proud. The only thing that I didn't do was fight in battle. Alfred insisted I was too young for that.

Fighting against the Vikings seemed to be almost constant, but however hard Alfred fought, he couldn't drive them out of Wessex. But neither had the Vikings defeated King Alfred. However, at Christmastide in the year 878, all looked as if it was about to change.

15

We had travelled to the town of Chippenham for

the religious holidays. After all the fighting, everyone was

resting and enjoying the festivities in the great hall.

Alfred had been feeling ill, with pains in his stomach

and had gone to his bed early to rest. It was then that

a lone soldier came running into the hall. He was soaked

from head to foot from the driving rain, his sword was

broken and his face was streaked with mud and blood.

"Vikings!" he yelled. "The Vikings are coming. We must flee

for our lives."

I ran to the royal chambers as fast as I could and woke Alfred from his sleep. No one had expected the Vikings to attack during the Christmastide festival and they took everyone by surprise. There was no time to prepare the soldiers for battle and we were greatly outnumbered.

"My lord," I cried, "we must leave while there is still time." Reluctantly, King Alfred agreed. He knew it was better to live and fight Guthrum another day than to throw away his life in a hopeless battle.

With my head bowed against the wind and the rain, I could barely see where we were going. All I could do was hold on tightly to the reins of my horse and stay as close to King Alfred as I could. We galloped away into the night, leaving Chippenham far behind us. "Where are we heading, my lord?" I called to him.

King Alfred turned his head towards me, a pained look on his face. "To the south-west," he replied. "We should be able to hide out there for a while." It felt strange to see King Alfred running away from a fight and to hear him talking of hiding. In all the time that I had known him, I had never known him to run. I could tell that he wasn't happy about it either. I could also tell that the pains in his stomach were troubling him and he was in no condition to fight a battle against a Viking warlord like Guthrum, vastly outnumbered and already battle-weary. We were lucky that we had received warning that the Vikings were coming.

After a couple of hours we finally reached the Somerset Levels, an area where the ground was wet and marshy. The horses slowed as they carefully picked their way across streams and waterlogged ground but King Alfred wasn't ready to stop.

"Keep close to me," the King called out to the other riders. "We need to find a place where Guthrum won't be able to find us." The Somerset Levels were a good place to hide. The vast area was a maze of rivers, streams, lakes and marshes. There were a few small villages and farms scattered on islands of raised land, but most of the area was deserted. Apart from the cold and damp, it seemed like an ideal place to rest and gather our forces.

King Alfred thought it might be better to spread out a little. "It's harder to spot a few men than it is to spot a group," he said. "We will meet up again in the morning, once we are rested." Some of the men took shelter in the ruins of an old farmhouse, but there wasn't enough room for everyone so we carried on through the marshes. As we waded through waist deep water with our horses following behind, I spotted the flickering of firelight in the darkness.

King Alfred had seen it too …

"That way," he said, pointing. "Towards the light."

The water was freezing cold and as we clambered out

I could hear my teeth chattering. A little way ahead of

us we could see a small huddle of buildings.

The flickering firelight we had spotted was coming from

the one nearest to us. I was so cold that even the orange

glow of light felt warming. Alfred knocked on the wooden

door with one gloved hand and waited.

CHAPTER 4
A PLACE TO REST

The door opened and a woman's face peered out at us, suspiciously. "Well!" she snapped. "What is it you want?" "Might we take shelter on this cold night?" Alfred asked politely. "Perhaps warm ourselves by your fire and rest our weary bones."

The woman looked us up and down as though we had crawled out of a swamp. Realising that was just what we had done, I couldn't help smiling. I don't know if it was my lord's polite words or my accidental smile, but the woman's face softened.
"First take your horses to shelter by the woodpile," she said. "Then you'd better come in."

The woman's house was simple but warm and comforting. A large fire pit stood in the middle of the room and the smoke from it snaked its way up to a small hole in the roof. In one corner was a table with a rough cloth thrown over it. Alfred took a seat by the fire and I helped remove his heavy chainmail and laid it out to dry.

The woman kindly brought us some dry clothes to put on. "May the good Lord bless your kindness," said King Alfred, putting on the dry clothes.

"I don't need blessing," said the woman. "But I do need to go and feed the pigs." Picking up a bucket of scraps, the woman headed to the door. "I've got some bread baking on the hearth," she said. "You make sure it doesn't burn." I'd noticed the flat breads as soon as we entered the house. They smelled delicious and my mouth watered at the sight of them.

22

"You arrange our clothes for drying," said Alfred, "and I'll keep my eye on the bread." As I set our clothes to dry, I could see Alfred was lost in thought. The Kingdom of Wessex had always been a stronghold against the Vikings but now things had changed for the worse. The king's soldiers had scattered and Guthrum was on the attack.

Just then, the sharp smell of burning reached my nose. "The bread!" I cried. Just then, the door burst open and the woman came in. Her face looked like thunder as she grabbed the iron skillet and took it away from the heat. "They're ruined," she shouted. "Even the pigs won't eat them now."

"Forgive me," said King Alfred. "I was lost in thought."

The woman was furious. For one moment I thought she was going to hit Alfred with her wooden bucket. Instead, she laid it down and scraped the burnt flat breads into the fire. "Luckily, I have enough to make more," she said.

The next morning I woke to find King Alfred dressed and sitting at the table with a bowl of porridge. "Eat up," he said, pointing his spoon at another bowlful ready for me. "We need to be on our way and leave this kind woman in peace."

As we rode away I turned to King Alfred and asked: "Why didn't you tell her who you were, my lord?" Alfred smiled. "The woman has a hard life," he said. "Yet she was kind enough to share her home and give us food and drink. What more could she have done by knowing I was King?"

24

CHAPTER 5

BECOMING GREAT

It would have been easy for Alfred to flee across sea

to safety in Gaul but he was determined to make

a final stand against Guthrum. After meeting up with

what was left of his army, we set up camp on the Isle of

Athelney. Linked to the mainland by a narrow causeway

only visible at low tide, there was an old fort there and it

didn't take long for it to be built up and strengthened.

The area was just above the waterline and surrounded by

dense marshland so that the camp would be hard to spot

until you were almost upon it. It would be hard for

the Vikings to attack in such marshy ground.

Guthrum, the Viking warlord, was certain he could defeat
Alfred and drive the Saxons out of the country once and
for all. He knew that Alfred was hiding out somewhere in
the Levels, but none of his scouts had managed to find
the camp. After spending winter in the fortified stronghold
of Chippenham, he decided to travel to the edge of
the marshes in the hope of finding and defeating Alfred.
Guthrum lined his army up on one of the highest points in
the Levels, ready for battle. As I helped Alfred into his
armour, I could hear the Vikings clashing their swords and
axes against their shields as they began moving towards
the marshes. It was a disturbing and frightening sound, sure
to put fear into the hearts of their enemies. Yet Alfred
ignored it and knelt in prayer in his tent. The Vikings were
getting steadily closer, but Alfred refused to move until his
prayers were finished. As soon as he had finished, he
reached for his weapons

26

Alfred insisted that I did not join the battle, but told me to climb to the top of a nearby hill. "From there you will be able to see all that happens," he said. "And you'll be safe from danger."

Looking down at the two armies, it seemed impossible to imagine how the Vikings could be defeated as they outnumbered the Saxon ranks by two to one, but I knew that Alfred would not give up. With a loud and valiant cry to arms, Alfred's soldiers lowered their shields and charged.

I will never forget the sights and sounds of that terrible battle; the crash and clatter of swords, axes and shields, or the screams and cries of the warriors. By the end, the field was awash with blood and bodies. Guthrum and his warriors turned and fled, but Alfred and his army pursued them. The Viking warlord and a few of his men made it back to the safety of Chippenham and shut and bolted the town's high wooden gates, but they knew they were defeated. After two weeks, the gates of the town opened and Guthrum stepped out. He dropped his battle axe onto the floor and held his hands out in surrender.

"What are you going to do, my lord?" I asked the king. "Will you put him to death?"

Looking down at me, Alfred shook his head. "Killing Guthrum will not end the fighting," he replied. "If I kill him, another warlord will rise up in his place. The Saxons and the Vikings need to find a way to live together in peace."

The Viking warlord
knelt before King Alfred.
"I surrender," he said.
"You are a great and
powerful warrior."

"You too are a great and powerful warrior," replied Alfred.

Guthrum shook his head. "I am a farmer," he said. "I came

here seeking enough land to farm so I could keep my

people fed." I could see Alfred thinking to himself for

a moment before replying. "If you agree to accept me as

your king then I will grant you enough land for you and

your people."

"So be it," Guthrum replied. "I will accept your kingship in

return for land for my people." And since that day, there

has been peace with the Vikings. King Alfred succeeded

in uniting the lands as a single country under his rule.

He was truly a great king.

Things to think about

1. What are Edwen's first impressions of Alfred?
2. Why does Edwen want to be his squire?
3. What do you think Alfred and Edwen learned when they stayed with the lady in the cottage?
4. Why does Alfred set up camp on the Isle of Athelney?
5. How does Alfred react when he captures Guthrum? Why do you think he shows compassion?

Write it yourself

This book retells the famous life of Alfred the Great and his defeat of the Viking Army. Now try to write your own retelling of a significant person's life or an event in history.

Plan your story before you begin to write it.

Start off with a story map:

- a beginning to introduce the characters and where and when your story is set (the setting);
- a problem that the main characters will need to fix in the story;
- an ending where the problems are resolved.

Get writing! Think about whose point of view you might tell the story from. Try to include geographical and historical details so that your readers get a sense of the time and place of your story, and think about the dialogue your characters would use.

Notes for parents and carers

Independent reading

The aim of independent reading is to read this book with ease. This series is designed to provide an opportunity for your child to read for pleasure and enjoyment. These notes are written for you to help your child make the most of this book.

About the book

This is a retelling of the story of how Alfred the Great and his Saxon army (849-899 CE) defeated the Viking invasion led by the mighty Viking warrior, Guthrum. While many historical facts are true, some characters such as the squire are made up.

Before reading

Ask your child why they have selected this book. Look at the title and blurb together. What do they think it will be about? Do they think they will like it?

During reading

Encourage your child to read independently. If they get stuck on a longer word, remind them that they can find syllable chunks that can be sounded out from left to right. They can also read on in the sentence and think about what would make sense.

After reading

Support comprehension by talking about the story. What happened?
Then help your child think about the messages in the book that go beyond the story, using the questions on the page opposite. Give your child a chance to respond to the story, asking:
Did you enjoy the story and why? Who was your favourite character?
What was your favourite part? What did you expect to happen at the end?

Franklin Watts
First published in Great Britain in 2019
by The Watts Publishing Group

Copyright © The Watts Publishing Group 2019
All rights reserved.

Series Editors: Jackie Hamley and Melanie Palmer
Series Advisors: Dr Sue Bodman and Glen Franklin
Series Designer: Peter Scoulding

A CIP catalogue record for this book is
available from the British Library.

ISBN 978 1 4451 6541 7 (hbk)
ISBN 978 1 4451 6542 4 (pbk)
ISBN 978 1 4451 7034 3 (library ebook)

Printed in China

Franklin Watts
An imprint of
Hachette Children's Group
Part of The Watts Publishing Group
Carmelite House
50 Victoria Embankment
London EC4Y 0DZ

An Hachette UK Company
www.hachette.co.uk

www.franklinwatts.co.uk